10 MINUTE SATs TESTS

SATs TESTS

3 subjects in 1

GRAMMAR, READING AND MATHS

YEAR 2

AGES 6–7

Scholastic Education, an imprint of Scholastic Ltd

Book End, Range Road, Witney, Oxfordshire, OX29 0YD

Registered office: Westfield Road, Southam, Warwickshire CV47 0RA

www.scholastic.co.uk

© 2019, Scholastic Ltd

1 2 3 4 5 6 7 8 9   9 0 1 2 3 4 5 6 7 8

British Library Cataloguing-in-Publication Data

A catalogue record for this book is available from the British Library.

ISBN 978-1407-18313-8

Printed and bound by Bell and Bain Ltd, Glasgow

Authors

Grammar, Punctuation and Spelling: Shelley Welsh

Reading: Helen Betts

Maths: Paul Hollin

Editorial

Rachel Morgan, Audrey Stokes, Suzanne Adams, Kate Pedlar, Kate Baxter, Gemma Smith

Design

Nicolle Thomas, Neil Salt, Dan Prescott/Couper Street Type Co. and Jayne Rawlings/Oxford Raw Design

Cover Illustration

Adam Linley @ Beehive Illustration

Illustration

Gaynor Barrs

Technical artwork

Darren Lingard/D'Avila Illustration Agency

Photographs

page 33: child reading, worawit_j/Shutterstock; finger on rose thorn, Tami Ann Wilcox/Shutterstock; page 34: girl sleeping, Duplass/Shutterstock

Contents

How to use this book

This book contains three grammar, punctuation and spelling tests, four reading tests and three sets of maths tests for Year 2. Each test contains SATs-style questions. The tests provide a wide coverage of the test frameworks for this age group.

Grammar, punctuation and spelling

It is intended that children will take around ten minutes to complete each part of each test (ten minutes for grammar and punctuation, and ten minutes for spelling). However, timings at this age are not strict, so allow your child as much time as they need.

Grammar and punctuation tests

Each test comprises ten questions, which amount to ten marks in total. Some questions require a selected response, where children select the correct answer from a list. Other questions require a constructed response, where children insert a word or punctuation mark, or write a short answer of their own.

Spelling tests

There are ten questions in each test, which amount to ten marks. Read each spelling number followed by *The word is...* Read the context sentence and then repeat *The word is...* Leave at least a 12-second gap between spellings. More information can be found on page 61.

Reading

Each test comprises a text followed by comprehension questions.
Test 1 and 2 have a short piece of text followed by related questions
immediately afterwards. Test 3 and 4 have a full text and then all the
questions follow. This mirrors the style of the two papers they will have
in the SATs test. It is intended that children will take approximately ten
minutes to complete each test. However, timings at this age are not
strict, so allow your child as much time as they need. Some questions
require a selected response, where children choose the correct answer
from several options. Other questions require a constructed response,
where children write a short or extended answer of their own.

Maths

It is intended that children will take approximately ten minutes to
complete each set of two tests. However, timings at this age are not
strict, so allow your child as much time as they need. Some questions
require a selected response, for example where children choose
the correct answer from several options. Other questions require a
constructed response, where children work out and write down their
own answer.

Marking the tests

A mark scheme and a progress chart are also included towards the end
of this book. After your child has completed a test, mark it and together
identify and practise any areas where your child is less confident. Ask
them to complete the next test at a later date, when you feel they have
had enough time to practise and improve.

Marks

1. Circle the **noun** in the sentence below.

We like bouncing on the trampoline.

1

2. Tick the name of the **punctuation mark** that should be used to complete each sentence below.

Sentence	Question mark	Exclamation mark
What time does the bell ring		
What a long day it's been		
Who is picking us up from school		

1

3. Tick the word that completes the sentence below.

I put on my coat _____ it was raining.

Tick **one**.

so	☐
because	☐
after	☐
and	☐

1

10 MINS

Marks

4. Add **two** letters to the word <u>tidy</u> to make a word that means <u>not tidy</u>.

Mum said our bedroom was very _____tidy.

1

5. Circle the **two adjectives** in the sentence below.

Dad put on his warm coat and went out into the frosty night.

1

6. Circle the **two** words that should start with a **capital letter** in the sentence below.

my hamster, who is one year old today, is called herbie.

1

KEEP IT GOING!

Marks

7. Which sentence below is a **command**?

Tick **one**.

It's almost time for the film to start. ☐

Where in the world have you been? ☐

How wonderful the weather was today! ☐

Bring me your plates when you have
finished eating. ☐

1

8. Tick the correct word to complete the sentence below.

Beth _____ enjoy the book.

Tick **one**.

did'nt ☐

d'int ☐

didn't' ☐

didn't ☐

1

10
MINS

Marks

9. Which sentence below is in the **past tense**?

Tick **one**.

Mum walks to work. ☐

Mum is walking to work. ☐

Mum walked to work. ☐

Mum is going to walk to work. ☐

1

10. Write a **question** you might ask your friend when they have come back from a holiday.

Remember to punctuate your sentence correctly.

_____

_____

1

Well done! END OF GRAMMAR & PUNCTUATION TEST 1!

		Marks
1.	Dad noticed a _____ in the glass.	

2. The bees were _____ around the flowers.

3. Ben gently _____ the little puppy.

4. Some _____ have moved in next door.

5. There was a loud _____ at the door.

6. Ravi told his sister to be _____.

7. I have broken the _____ on my bike.

8. Marcus always _____ the shopping for his mum.

9. Gran is taking us to a _____ show next week.

10. Ciara _____ her brother's present.

10

Well done! END OF SPELLING TEST 1!

Marks

1. What type of word is underlined in the sentence below?

Dad <u>peeled</u> the carrots and potatoes.

Tick **one**.

a noun ☐

an adjective ☐

an adverb ☐

a verb ☐

1

2. Which **punctuation mark** is missing from the sentence below?

Freds new football is blue, white and green.

Tick **one**.

a comma ☐

a full stop ☐

an apostrophe ☐

an exclamation mark ☐

1

3. Add the missing **comma** to the sentence below.

Mum placed the apples bananas and pears in the fruit bowl.

1

Marks

4. Look at the parts of the words that are in bold.

sad**ness**   play**ful**   care**less**   sure**ly**

What is the name for this part of the word?

Tick **one**.

a prefix ☐

a verb ☐

a suffix ☐

an adverb ☐

1

5. Add the missing **punctuation mark** to the end of the sentence below.

Where do you go to school ___

1

6. Choose **one** word that completes the sentence below. Write the word on the line in the sentence.

| that | if | before | but |

Our teacher said we could go out to play

_____ we behaved well.

1

10 MINS

Marks

7. Circle the word that shows the sentence below is in the **present tense**.

The weather today is cold, wet and windy.

1

8. What is the **noun phrase** in the sentence below?

Yesterday, I drew a picture of a huge elephant with a long trunk.

Tick **one**.

I drew a picture ☐

Yesterday ☐

a huge elephant with a long trunk ☐

drew ☐

1

KEEP IT GOING!

**10
MINS**

9. The verbs in the sentence below should all be in the **present tense**.

Circle **one** word that needs to be changed.

I tried every day to practise my times tables but sometimes it is hard.

1

10. The final **punctuation mark** is missing from the sentence below.

What kind of sentence is it?

How fabulous it was to watch the fireworks last night

Tick **one**.

a statement ☐

a question ☐

a command ☐

an exclamation ☐

1

Well done! END OF GRAMMAR & PUNCTUATION TEST 2!

Marks

1. Mum wore a _____ hat to the wedding.

2. We stroked the _____.

3. Tom heard a bang in the _____ of the night.

4. At the zoo, we took a picture of the _____.

5. We rushed to the _____ when we heard the bell.

6. The _____ rang twice, then stopped.

7. Ahmed _____ happily towards the park.

8. Our teacher asked us to complete one _____ of the test.

9. The pirates buried the _____ at the bottom of the sea.

10. My new leather shoes are very good _____.

10

Well done! END OF SPELLING TEST 2!

Marks

1. Insert the **two** missing **full stops** in the sentences below.

I play tennis after school Bethan is my partner

1

2. What type of word is underlined in the sentence below?

Gregor <u>wrote</u> his name at the top of the page.

Tick one.

a noun ☐

an adjective ☐

a verb ☐

an adverb ☐

1

3. Circle the **adverb** in the sentence below.

Tia carefully mixed the eggs, butter and flour.

1

10 MINS

Marks

4. Tick the sentence below that is a **statement**.

Tick **one**.

I like milk on my cornflakes. ☐

Do you like milk on your cornflakes? ☐

Pour some milk on your cornflakes. ☐

How crunchy these cornflakes are! ☐

1

5. Write the words <u>have not</u> as **one** word using an **apostrophe**.

I <u>have not</u> seen my uncle for many years.

↑

☐

1

6. Which sentence below tells you what Claire is doing <u>now</u>?

Tick **one**.

Claire went fishing with her grandad. ☐

Claire is watching a film with her gran. ☐

Claire was writing a letter to her grandad. ☐

Claire helped her gran wash the dishes. ☐

1

10 MINS

Marks

7. Draw a line to match each word to the correct **suffix** to make a new word.

One has been done for you.

Word	Suffix
wonder	ment
hope	ness
kind	less
enjoy	ful

1

8. Circle **two** words in the sentence below that should start with a **capital letter**.

sam is going to scotland for the summer.

1

KEEP IT GOING!

18

Marks

9. Draw a line to match each sentence on the left to its correct function on the right.

What lovely new gloves you have!		statement
I wish I had some new gloves.		command
Tell me where you bought them.		question
Can I borrow them please?		exclamation

1

10. Rewrite the two sentences below as one, using **one** of the words below to join them.

Write your sentence on the line.

| and | but | so | if |

Josef likes peas. He doesn't like carrots.

_____

_____

1

Well done! END OF GRAMMAR & PUNCTUATION TEST 3!

19

Marks

1. We had to _____ a long distance to the house.

2. Mum _____ the cream for the cake.

3. I bought some _____ for Gran's birthday present.

4. My baby brother _____ when he is hungry.

5. Grace packed her _____ for the sleepover.

6. Our neighbours have just sold _____ house.

7. I _____ to Pippa's party invitation.

8. Our teacher showed us a _____ in our science lesson.

9. When _____ had stopped talking, we went out to play.

10. Two _____ in our school have a new teacher this year.

Well done! END OF SPELLING TEST 3!

10

Barty

Barty loved ketchup. He had it with everything.

He had it for breakfast. He had it for lunch. He had it for dinner.

Barty's family thought he was crazy. "Crazy for ketchup!" they all said.

Example question

a. What did Barty have with everything?

ketchup

I. **Find** and **copy two** words for the meals Barty had.

1. _____ 2. _____

_____

Marks

1

2. Why did Barty's family think he was crazy?

Tick **one**.

He loved breakfast so much. ☐

He loved ketchup so much. ☐

He loved them all so much. ☐

1

One day, Barty's friend Cedric invited Barty to a sleepover at his house. Barty was really excited.

When he got there, he raced up to Cedric's room and they played games, cards and puzzles. Then it was time for dinner.

Cedric's family was having one of Barty's favourites – grass pizza!

3. Find and **copy one** word that shows Barty was pleased to be going to Cedric's house.

Marks

_____

_____

1

4. What does *he raced* tell you about how Barty moved?

Tick **one**.

He moved carefully. ☐

He moved sleepily. ☐

He moved quickly. ☐

1

5. What were Cedric's family having for dinner?

_____

1

"Can I have the ketchup, please?" asked Barty.

"Oh. I don't think we have any," said Cedric's mum.

NO KETCHUP! What was Barty to do?

First, he watched everyone else eat. Then he drank all his drink. Then he thought he would cry. Finally, he tried one little piece.

Then he tried another one and another.

6. How do you think Barty felt when Cedric's mum said they had no ketchup?

Circle **one**.

| hungry | rude | upset |

Marks

1

---

7. What did Barty do after he drank his drink?

Tick **one**.

He watched everyone eat.

He asked for some ketchup. ☐

He tried one piece of pizza. ☐

KEEP IT GOING!

1

And then he asked for seconds. It was quite good really, even if it needed ketchup.

When he got home the next day, everyone thought Barty was cured of his ketchup craze!

But the next time he slept over at Cedric's, there was one thing he didn't forget to pack...

Marks

8. What did Barty think of the pizza in the end?

_____

_____

1

9. Choose **one** statement that sums up the end of the story.

Tick **one.**

Barty was cured of his ketchup craze. ☐

Barty still wanted ketchup with everything. ☐

Barty decided he did not like sleepovers. ☐

1

10. What do you think Barty _didn't forget to pack_ the next time he slept over at Cedric's?

_____

1

Well done! END OF READING TEST 1!

Reading
Test 2

10 MINS

Plastic bottle piggy bank

You can turn old plastic bottles into new and exciting things. Try this idea to make a piggy bank.

You will need:
- a clean plastic bottle
- pink paint
- pink paper
- scissors
- glue
- a pink pipe cleaner
- a black felt-tipped pen

Marks

1. What can you make by doing this activity?

_____

_____

1

2. **Find** and **copy two** pink things you need for this activity.

1. _____   2. _____

1

3. Why do you think the writer used the word *exciting*?

Tick one.

so you know what you need ☐

so you want to try the activity ☐

to show you what to do ☐

1

10 MINS

Ask a grown-up to help you with any cutting!

Step 1: Cut out a hole in the long side of the plastic bottle. The hole should be big enough to fit coins through.

Step 2: Paint your plastic bottle pink all over and leave it to dry.

4. Find and **copy one** word that tells you what you should ask a grown-up for help with.

Marks

1

_____

_____

5. How big does the hole need to be?

Tick one.

the length of the bottle ☐

the size of a paintbrush ☐

big enough for coins ☐

1

KEEP IT GOING!

10 MINS

Step 3: Cut a strip of pink paper into four rectangles. Cut out two triangles for the ears and a circle for the snout.

Step 4: Roll the rectangles into tubes. Leave them to the side until the glue has set. These will be your piggy bank legs.

6. Draw lines to match the shape with the part of the pig.

Marks

Shape	Part
triangles	snout
rectangles	ears
circle	legs

1

7. Which of these things is **not** needed for Steps 3 and 4? Circle **one**.

pink paint   scissors   glue

1

Step 5: Wrap the pipe cleaner around your finger to make it into a curly tail.

Step 6: Use glue to stick the ears, legs, snout and tail onto the painted bottle.

Step 7: Draw a pair of eyes on your piggy bank.

Now you can start saving!

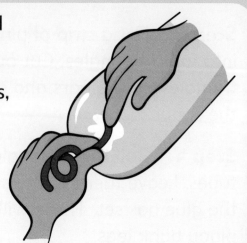

8. What should you wrap the pipe cleaner around to make the tail?

_____

_____

9. Find and **copy one** word that tells you the pig's tail is <u>not straight</u>.

_____

_____

10. Number the sentences 1–4 to put the steps in order.

Make the tail.	
Paint the bottle pink.	
Draw the eyes.	
Make the ears, snout and legs.	

Marks

1

1

1

Well done! END OF READING TEST 2!

Have you heard the moon?

Have you heard the moon?
Have you heard it sigh
as it sits collecting stardust
on its moonshelf in the sky?

Have you heard the sun?
Have you heard it sing
and shine the air with promises
of what the day may bring?

Have you heard the rain?
Have you heard it cry
sobbing its broken heart out
when its tears fill the sky?

Have you heard the wind?
Have you heard it moan?
Its wicked wind chill factor
will chill you to the bone.

Have you heard the sea?
Have you heard it roar
as it rolls and swells and slowly
waves goodbye towards the shore?

By Craig Bradley

10 MINS

Marks

1. **Find** and **copy one** word to describe the sound made by the moon.

_____

_____

1

2. What does the poet say the moon collects?

_____

_____

1

3. Look at the third verse. How does the rain feel?

Circle **one**.

hopeful   sad   bored

1

KEEP IT GOING!

Marks

4. Look at the fourth verse. **Find** and **copy one** word that has a similar meaning to <u>horrible</u>.

_____

_____

1

5. *Its wicked wind chill factor*
will chill you to the bone.

Circle **one** phrase that means the same as *chill you*.

| make you angry | amaze you | make you cold |

1

6. *as it rolls and swells and slowly*
waves goodbye towards the shore

What is happening in this part of the poem?

Tick **one**.

The tide is going out. ☐

The sea is very quiet. ☐

The waves are crying. ☐

1

Marks

7. Tick **true** or **false** for each statement below.

	True	False
The first verse is all about the stars.		
In the poem, the wind makes a moaning sound.		
In the poem, the sea moves quickly.		

1

8. Look at the whole poem. Choose **one** statement that best sums up what it is about.

Tick one.

the water cycle

the seasons of the year

the world all around us

1

9. Look at the second verse. What kind of mood does the poet think the sun creates? Explain your answer.

_____

_____

_____

2

Well done! END OF READING TEST 3!

Your brilliant brain

Your body is made of lots of parts that work together in very clever ways. One of the most brilliant parts is your brain! Without it, you would not be able to think, talk, move, hear, see or read.

Sending messages

Your brain is joined to every part of your body by tiny paths called nerves. Messages go along your nerves, to and from your brain. To pick a flower, your brain sends a message to your hand telling it to pick the flower. If you see a thorn, your brain sends a message to be careful!

Memory

Your memory is how your brain holds information. Your memory will never get full because your brain can remember so much information. The brain of an eight-year-old holds more information than a million books!

Time to rest

Sleeping gives your brain a rest. Some parts of your brain shut down while you sleep. The parts that make dreams are busy. Some people have brains that stay more awake. Sometimes they talk or walk in their sleep.

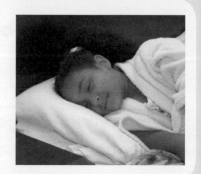

Marks

1. Which of these words has the same meaning as *brilliant*? Circle **one**.

amazing   puzzling   enormous

1

2. Look at the first paragraph. **Find** and **copy two** words that tell you what the brain helps us to do.

1. _____   2. _____

1

3. What is the name for the tiny paths that carry messages in your body?

_____

1

4. What message does the brain send to your hand if you see a thorn?

_____

1

Marks

5. How does your brain hold information?

Tick one.

in your dreams ☐

in your nerves ☐

in your memory ☐

1

---

6. *The brain of an eight-year-old holds more information than a million books!*

Why do you think the writer has included this fact?
Write **two** reasons.

1. _____

2. _____

2

---

7. Why do some people talk or walk in their sleep?

Tick one.

Their brain has shut down. ☐

Their brain is still awake. ☐

They are busy dreaming. ☐

1

10 MINS

8. Tick **true** or **false** for each statement below.

Marks

	True	False
The nerves join the brain to the rest of your body.		
Your memory is full by the time you are eight years old.		
Reading and talking help your brain to rest.		

1

9. Look at this new fact. Which section of the text would it best fit into?

<u>The nerves in your body are 70 kilometres long!</u>

Tick **one**.

Sending messages ☐

Memory ☐

Time to rest ☐

1

Well done! END OF READING TEST 4!

Marks

1. $3 + 5 = \boxed{}$

1

2. $36 + 10 + 10 = \boxed{}$

1

3. $\boxed{} - 7 = 8$

1

10 MINS

Marks

4. $5 \times \boxed{} = 20$

1

5. $\dfrac{1}{2}$ of 22 = $\boxed{}$

1

6. $44 - 25 =$ $\boxed{}$

1

Well done! END OF MATHS SET A TEST 1!

10 MINS

	Marks

1. Shade $\frac{1}{4}$ of this shape.

1

2. John makes 15 using these shapes for tens and ones.

John makes a new number.

What is John's new number?

1

10 MINS

Marks

3. Draw a line to match each shape to its name.

One has been done for you.

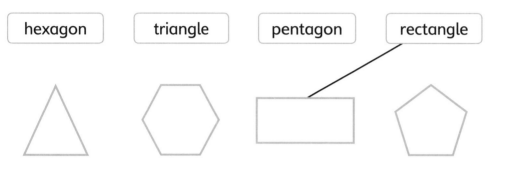

| hexagon | triangle | pentagon | rectangle |

1

4. The chart shows traffic passing the school gates.

Transport	Bike	Bus	Car	Lorry
Number	⊞⊞ ⊞⊞ ‖	‖	⊞⊞ ‖	‖‖

Complete the bar chart.

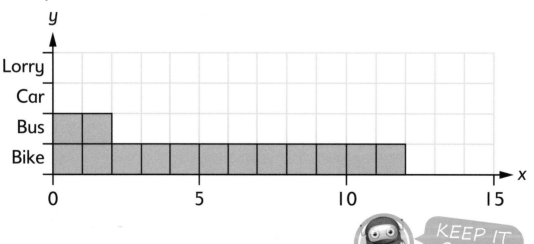

1

KEEP IT GOING!

10 MINS

5. Leanne has these coins in her purse.

If she buys a pen for 80p, how much money will she have left?

Marks

| | p |

1

---

6. The school cook makes one mini pizza for each child in school.

8 mini pizzas fit on 1 tray.

He cooks 10 trays of pizzas.

If 73 children have pizza for lunch, how many pizzas will be left over?

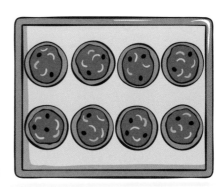

 Show your working

pizzas

2

Well done! END OF MATHS SET A TEST 2!

Maths
Set B Test 1: Arithmetic

10 MINS

Marks

1. 9 − 6 = [ ]

1

2. 5 + 5 + 5 = [ ]

1

3. [ ] × 6 = 60

1

10 MINS

Marks

4. $103 - 4 =$ ☐

1

5. $40 \div 5 =$ ☐

1

6. $56 + 35 =$ ☐

1

Well done! END OF MATHS SET B TEST 1!

10 MINS

Marks

1. Write these numbers in order, from **smallest** to **largest**.

| 6 | 75 | 49 | 28 | 96 |

| | | | | |

smallest   **largest**

1

2. A maths lesson starts at this time.

What time does the clock show?

Circle **one**.

| quarter to 10 | half past 9 |

| half past 8 | quarter past 9 |

1

KEEP IT GOING!

3. Mia does an addition.

$$32 + 45 = 77$$

Write a subtraction that shows Mia is correct.

[ ] − [ ] = [ ]

Marks

1

---

4. There are 12 counters.

Lily takes half of them, and then Josh takes half of the left-over counters.

How many counters does Josh have?

 Show your working

[ ] counters

2

45

5. Write instructions to guide a robot from A to B. The first two have been done for you.

A  B

Marks

Turn right 90°

Forward 4

Well done! END OF MATHS SET B TEST 2!

46

2

Marks

1. $3 + 3 + 3 =$ ⬚

1

2. $65 - 1 =$ ⬚

1

3. $7 \times 10 =$ ⬚

1

10 MINS

Marks

4. $13 - \boxed{} = 7$

1

5. $\dfrac{1}{4}$ of $8 = \boxed{}$

1

6. $33 + 28 = \boxed{}$

Well done! END OF MATHS SET C TEST 1!

1

Maths

Set C Test 2: Reasoning

Marks

1. Here is a pattern.

Circle the next pattern in the sequence.

 or

1

2. Shade the fractions of the shapes.

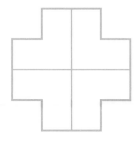 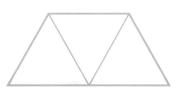 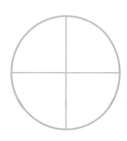

shade $\frac{1}{2}$ shade $\frac{2}{3}$ shade $\frac{3}{4}$

1

49

Marks

3. The children in Class 2 choose their favourite fruit. The chart shows the results.

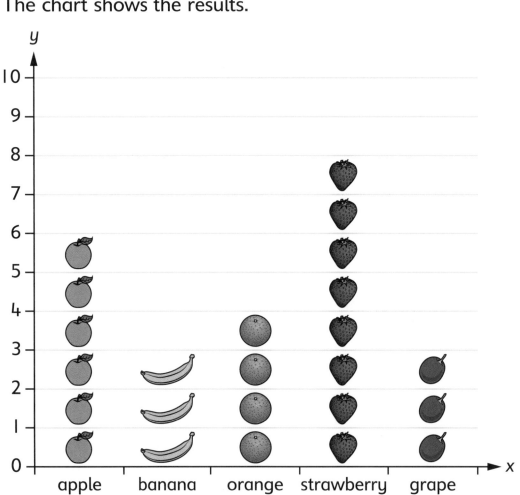

a. How many more children choose strawberries than bananas?

children

1

b. Another child joins Class 2.

She chooses apple as her favourite fruit.

Add this information to the chart.

1

10 MINS

Marks

4. Write the correct numbers in the boxes on the number line.

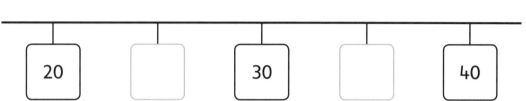

| 20 | | 30 | | 40 |

1

5. Admission to a school fair is 10p for children and 20p for adults.

Natalie and her two younger brothers go with their mum and dad.

How much will they have to pay?

 Show your working

p

2

Well done! END OF MATHS SET C TEST 2!

Answers
Grammar and Punctuation

Q	Mark scheme for Grammar and Punctuation Test 1	Marks
1	**Award 1 mark** if 'trampoline' is circled. **Grammar essentials**: A noun is a naming word for a person, place, thing, animal, idea or concept.	1
2	**Award 1 mark** for each row ticked correctly: Grammar and punctuation essentials below table	1

Award 1 mark for each row ticked correctly:

Sentence	Question mark	Exclamation mark
What time does the bell ring	✔	
What a long day it's been		✔
Who is picking us up from school	✔	

Grammar and punctuation essentials: A question always starts with a capital letter and ends with a question mark. A question asks you to do something. An exclamation sentence starts with a capital letter, begins with 'How' or 'What', contains a verb and ends with an exclamation mark.

Q		Marks
3	**Award 1 mark** if 'because' is ticked. **Grammar essentials**: 'Because' is a subordinating conjunction which introduces a subordinate clause, for example: '...because it was raining'.	1
4	**Award 1 mark** for: 'Mum said our bedroom was very **un**tidy.'. **Grammar essentials**: A prefix is a string of letters added to the beginning of a word to turn it into another word. It does not alter the spelling of the word it is joined to. Adding the prefix 'un' to 'tidy' makes it opposite in meaning.	1
5	**Award 1 mark** if 'warm' and 'frosty' are circled. **Grammar essentials**: An adjective can come before the noun, as here, to modify it, or after the verb 'to be' as its complement.	1
6	**Award 1 mark** if 'my' and 'herbie' are circled. **Punctuation essentials**: A sentence starts with a capital letter. Proper nouns, such as a person's or animal's name, also start with a capital letter.	1
7	**Award 1 mark** if 'Bring me your plates when you have finished eating.' is ticked. **Grammar and punctuation essentials**: A command is a sentence that tells you to do something and can end with a full stop or an exclamation mark.	1
8	**Award 1 mark** if 'didn't' is ticked. **Punctuation essentials**: An apostrophe can be used to indicate a missing letter or letters.	1
9	**Award 1 mark** if 'Mum walked to work.' is ticked. **Grammar essentials**: The past tense describes an event that has happened.	1
10	**Award 1 mark** for a suitable question starting with a capital letter and ending with a question mark, for example: 'Did you have a nice time?' **Grammar and punctuation essentials**: A question always starts with a capital letter and ends with a question mark.	1
	Total	10

Q	Mark scheme for Grammar and Punctuation Test 2	Marks
1	**Award 1 mark** if 'a verb' is ticked. **Grammar essentials**: A verb is a word that names an action, a state of being or a feeling.	1
2	**Award 1 mark** if 'an apostrophe' is ticked. **Punctuation essentials**: An apostrophe can be used to show possession, as here. For singular possession, it comes between the final letter of the word and the letter 's'.	1
3	**Award 1 mark** for: 'Mum placed the apples**,** bananas and pears in the fruit bowl.' **Punctuation essentials**: Commas can be used to separate items in a list. In lists like these, there is no comma before the word 'and'.	1
4	**Award 1 mark** if 'a suffix' is ticked. **Grammar essentials**: A suffix is a letter or string of letters added to the end of a word to turn it into another word.	1
5	**Award 1 mark** for the correct insertion of a question mark: 'Where do you go to school**?**' **Punctuation essentials**: A question mark comes at the end of a question.	1
6	**Award 1 mark** for: 'Our teacher said we could go out to play **if** we behaved well.'. **Grammar essentials**: A subordinating conjunction introduces a subordinate clause.	1
7	**Award 1 mark** if 'is' is circled. **Grammar essentials**: 'is' is the present tense, third person singular, of the verb 'to be'. A verb is a word that names an action, a state of being or a feeling.	1
8	**Award 1 mark** if 'a huge elephant with a long trunk' is ticked. **Grammar essentials**: A noun phrase is a group of words that adds more information about a noun. The noun is the most important word in the phrase.	1
9	**Award 1 mark** if 'tried' is circled. **Grammar essentials**: The past tense describes an event that has happened. The present tense describes an event or a habit, as here, that is happening now.	1
10	**Award 1 mark** if 'an exclamation' is ticked. **Punctuation essentials**: An exclamation sentence starts with a capital letter, begins with 'How' or 'What', contains a verb and ends with an exclamation mark.	1
	Total	10

Q	Mark scheme for Grammar and Punctuation Test 3	Marks
1	**Award 1 mark** for: 'I play tennis after school. Bethan is my partner.' **Punctuation essentials**: A full stop comes at the end of a sentence.	1
2	**Award 1 mark** if 'a verb' is ticked. **Grammar essentials**: A verb is a word that names an action, a state of being or a feeling.	1
3	**Award 1 mark** if 'carefully' is circled. **Grammar essentials**: An adverb can give more information about the verb in a sentence.	1
4	**Award 1 mark** if 'I like milk on my cornflakes' is ticked. **Grammar and punctuation essentials**: A statement is a sentence that tells you something. It starts with a capital letter and ends with a full stop.	1
5	**Award 1 mark** for: 'haven't' spelled correctly, with the apostrophe placed between 'n' and 't'. **Punctuation essentials**: An apostrophe can be used in a contraction to indicate a missing letter or letters.	1
6	**Award 1 mark** if 'Claire is watching a film with her gran.' is ticked. **Grammar essentials**: An event in the present can be indicated using either the simple present tense or the present progressive tense, as here.	1
7	**Award 1 mark** for all three correct: wonderful, kindness, enjoyment. **Grammar essentials**: A suffix is a string of letters added to the end of a word to turn it into another word.	1
8	**Award 1 mark** if 'sam' and 'scotland' are circled. **Punctuation essentials**: Proper nouns, such as people's names and names of countries, start with a capital letter.	1
9	**Award 1 mark** for all four correct: What lovely new gloves you have! – exclamation I wish I had some new gloves. – statement Tell me where you bought them. – command Can I borrow them please? – question **Grammar and punctuation essentials**: An exclamation sentence starts with 'How' or 'What', contains a verb and ends with an exclamation mark. A statement tells you something and usually ends with a full stop. A command is a sentence that tells you to do something and can end with a full stop or an exclamation mark. A question asks you to do something and ends with a question mark.	1
10	**Award 1 mark** for: 'Josef likes peas **but** he doesn't like carrots.' **Grammar essentials**: A co-ordinating conjunction (such as 'but', 'or' or 'and') can link two phrases or clauses together as an equal pair.	1
	Total	10

Answers
Reading

Q	Mark scheme for Reading Test 1: Barty	Marks
1	**Award 1 mark** for any two of: breakfast, lunch, dinner	1
2	**Award 1 mark** for: He loved ketchup so much.	1
3	**Award 1 mark** for: excited	1
4	**Award 1 mark** for: He moved quickly.	1
5	**Award 1 mark** for: (grass) pizza OR one of Barty's favourites	1
6	**Award 1 mark** for: upset	1
7	**Award 1 mark** for: He tried one piece of pizza.	1
8	**Award 1 mark** for an appropriate answer, for example: It was quite good/nice. OR He quite liked it. OR He thought it needed ketchup.	1
9	**Award 1 mark** for: Barty still wanted ketchup with everything.	1
10	**Award 1 mark** for: ketchup	1
	Total	10

Q	Mark scheme for Reading Test 2: Plastic bottle piggy bank	Marks
1	**Award 1 mark** for: a piggy bank	1
2	**Award 1 mark** for any two of: paint, paper, pipe cleaner	1
3	**Award 1 mark** for: so you want to try the activity	1
4	**Award 1 mark** for: (any) cutting OR using scissors	1
5	**Award 1 mark** for: big enough for coins	1
6	**Award 1 mark** for all three matched correctly: triangles — snout, rectangles — ears, circle — legs	1
7	**Award 1 mark** for: pink paint	1
8	**Award 1 mark** for: your finger	1
9	**Award 1 mark** for: curly	1
10	**Award 1 mark** for all four sentences in the correct order: Make the tail. — 3; Paint the bottle pink. — 1; Draw the eyes. — 4; Make the ears, snout and legs. — 2	1
	Total	10

Q	Mark scheme for Reading Test 3: Have you heard the moon?	Marks
1	**Award 1 mark** for: sigh	1
2	**Award 1 mark** for: stardust	1
3	**Award 1 mark** for: sad	1
4	**Award 1 mark** for: wicked	1
5	**Award 1 mark** for: make you cold	1
6	**Award 1 mark** for: The tide is going out.	1
7	**Award 1 mark** for all three ticked correctly:	1
8	**Award 1 mark** for: the world all around us	1
9	**Award 2 marks** for suitable answer, for example: A happy mood because it is singing. OR A happy mood because it is shining and so brightens the day. OR A hopeful mood because it brings promises. **Award 1 mark** for an appropriate mood with no explanation.	2

For Q7:

Statement	True	False
The first verse is all about the stars.		✔
In the poem, the wind makes a moaning sound.	✔	
In the poem, the sea moves quickly.		✔

Total 10

Q	Mark scheme for Reading Test 4: Your brilliant brain	Marks
1	**Award 1 mark** for: amazing	1
2	**Award 1 mark** for any two of: think, talk, move, hear, see, read	1
3	**Award 1 mark** for: nerve(s)	1
4	**Award 1 mark** for: be careful!	1
5	**Award 1 mark** for: in your memory	1
6	**Award 2 marks** for two plausible reasons, for example: 1. To give you a better idea of how much information the brain can hold. OR To make it easier to understand how much information the brain can hold. 2. To make it more interesting to a child reader as it shows that even when you're young you know a lot. **Award 1 mark** for one appropriate reason.	2
7	**Award 1 mark** for: Their brain is still awake.	1
8	**Award 1 mark** for all three ticked correctly:	1
9	**Award 1 mark** for: Sending messages	1

For Q8:

	True	False
The nerves join the brain to the rest of your body.	✔	
Your memory is full by the time you are eight years old.		✔
Reading and talking help your brain to rest.		✔

Total 10

Answers

Maths

Q	Mark scheme for Maths Set A Test 1: Arithmetic	Marks
1	8	1
2	56	1
3	15	1
4	4	1
5	11	1
6	19	1
	Total	6

Q	Mark scheme for Maths Set A Test 2: Reasoning	Marks
1	Any one rectangle shaded, for example:	1
2	32	1
3		1
4		1

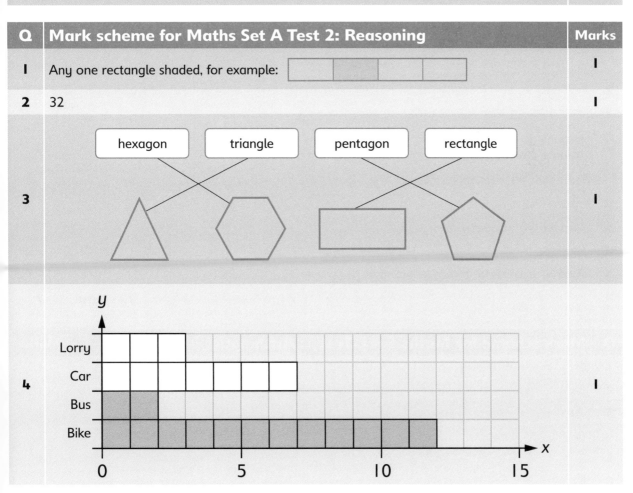

Q	Mark scheme for Maths Set A Test 2: Reasoning continued	Marks
5	40p	1
6	7 pizzas **Award 1 mark** for a correct method but with a maximum of one arithmetical error.	2
	Total	7

Q	Mark scheme for Maths Set B Test 1: Arithmetic	Marks
1	3	1
2	15	1
3	10	1
4	99	1
5	8	1
6	91	1
	Total	6

Q	Mark scheme for Maths Set B Test 2: Reasoning	Marks
1	6, 28, 49, 75, 96	1
2	half past 9	1
3	77 – 45 = 32 OR 77 – 32 = 45	1
4	3 counters **Award 1 mark** for a correct method but with a maximum of one arithmetical error.	2
5	Turn right 90° (accept Turn left 270°) Forward 2 Turn left 90° (accept Turn right 270°) Forward 1 **Award 1 mark** for three correct steps.	2
	Total	7

Q	Mark scheme for Maths Set C Test 1: Arithmetic	Marks
1	9	1
2	64	1
3	70	1
4	6	1
5	2	1
6	61	1
	Total	6

The first pattern – four triangles and five circles:

1

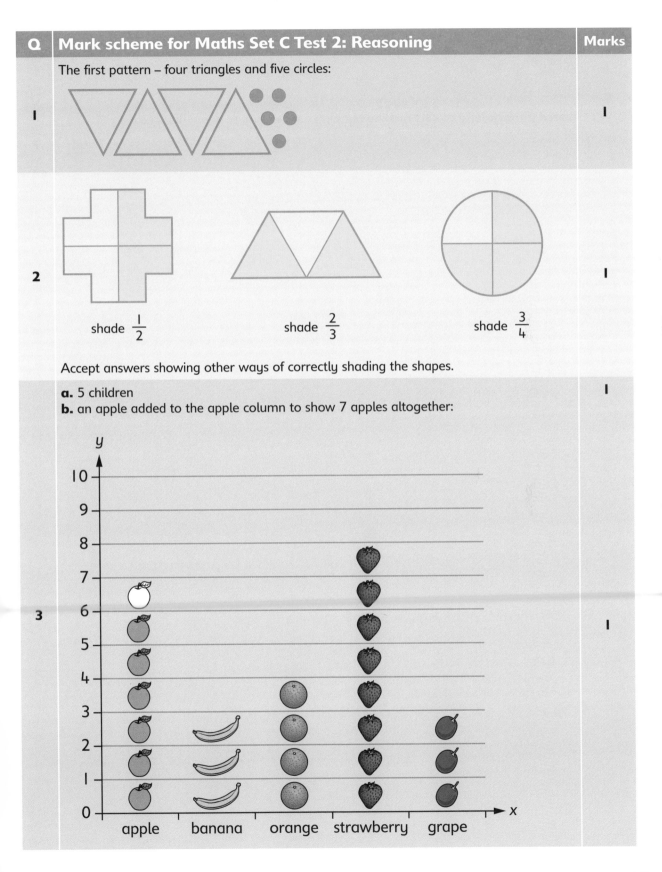

1

2

shade $\frac{1}{2}$ 　　　　 shade $\frac{2}{3}$ 　　　　 shade $\frac{3}{4}$

1

Accept answers showing other ways of correctly shading the shapes.

---

a. 5 children

b. an apple added to the apple column to show 7 apples altogether:

3

1

1

Q	Mark scheme for Maths Set C Test 2: Reasoning continued	Marks
4	20 **25** 30 **35** 40	1
5	70p **Award 1 mark** for a correct method but with a maximum of one arithmetical error.	2
	Total	7

How to administer the spelling tests

There are three short spelling tests in this book. Each test consists of ten questions; you should allow your child as much time as they need to complete them.

Read the instructions in the box below. The instructions are similar to the ones given in the National Curriculum tests. This will familiarise children with the style and format of the tests and show them what to expect.

> *Listen carefully to the instructions I am going to give you.*
>
> *I am going to read ten sentences to you. Each sentence on your answer sheet has a missing word. Listen carefully to the missing word and write it in the space provided, making sure you spell the word correctly.*
>
> *I will read the word, then the word within the sentence, then repeat the word a third time.*
>
> *Do you have any questions?*

Read the spellings as follows:

- Give the question number, 'Spelling 1'
- Say, 'The word is...'
- Read the whole sentence to show the word in context
- Repeat, 'The word is...'

Leave at least a 12-second gap between each spelling.

At the end re-read all ten questions. Then say, 'This is the end of the test. Please put down your pencil or pen.'

Each correct answer should be awarded **1 mark**.

Spelling test transcripts

Spelling Test 1

Spelling 1: The word is **crack**.
Dad noticed a **crack** in the glass.
The word is **crack**.

Spelling 2: The word is **buzzing**.
The bees were **buzzing** around the flowers.
The word is **buzzing**.

Spelling 3: The word is **patted**.
Ben gently **patted** the little puppy.
The word is **patted**.

Spelling 4: The word is **people**.
Some **people** have moved in next door.
The word is **people**.

Spelling 5: The word is **knock**.
There was a loud **knock** at the door.
The word is **knock**.

Spelling 6: The word is **quiet**.
Ravi told his sister to be **quiet**.
The word is **quiet**.

Spelling 7: The word is **pedal**.
I have broken the **pedal** on my bike.
The word is **pedal**.

Spelling 8: The word is **carries**.
Marcus always **carries** the shopping for his mum.
The word is **carries**.

Spelling 9: The word is **magic**.
Gran is taking us to a **magic** show next week.
The word is **magic**.

Spelling 10: The word is **wrapped**.
Ciara **wrapped** her brother's present.
The word is **wrapped**.

Spelling Test 2

Spelling 1: The word is **fancy**.
Mum wore a **fancy** hat to the wedding.
The word is **fancy**.

Spelling 2: The word is **puppies**.
We stroked the **puppies**.
The word is **puppies**.

Spelling 3: The word is **middle**.
Tom heard a bang in the **middle** of the night.
The word is **middle**.

Spelling 4: The word is **monkeys**.
At the zoo, we took a picture of the **monkeys**.
The word is **monkeys**.

Spelling 5: The word is **playground**.
We rushed to the **playground** when we heard the bell.
The word is **playground**.

Spelling 6: The word is **telephone**.
The **telephone** rang twice, then stopped.
The word is **telephone**.

Spelling 7: The word is **skipped**.
Ahmed **skipped** happily towards the park.
The word is **skipped**.

Spelling 8: The word is **section**.
Our teacher asked us to complete one **section** of the test.
The word is **section**.

Spelling 9: The word is **treasure**.
The pirates buried the **treasure** at the bottom of the sea.
The word is **treasure**.

Spelling 10: The word is **quality**.
My new leather shoes are very good **quality**.
The word is **quality**.

Spelling Test 3

Spelling 1: The word is **travel**.
We had to **travel** a long distance to the house.
The word is **travel**.

Spelling 2: The word is **whipped**.
Mum **whipped** the cream for the cake.
The word is **whipped**.

Spelling 3: The word is **fudge**.
I bought some **fudge** for Gran's birthday present.
The word is **fudge**.

Spelling 4: The word is **cries**.
My baby brother **cries** when he is hungry.
The word is **cries**.

Spelling 5: The word is **clothes**.
Grace packed her **clothes** for the sleepover.
The word is **clothes**.

Spelling 6: The word is **their**.
Our neighbours have just sold **their** house.
The word is **their**.

Spelling 7: The word is **replied**.
I **replied** to Pippa's party invitation.
The word is **replied**.

Spelling 8: The word is **fossil**.
Our teacher showed us a **fossil** in our science lesson.
The word is **fossil**.

Spelling 9: The word is **everybody**.
When **everybody** had stopped talking, we went out to play.
The word is **everybody**.

Spelling 10: The word is **classes**.
Two **classes** in our school have a new teacher this year.
The word is **classes**.

Progress chart

Fill in your score in the table below to see how well you've done.

Test number	Score	Percentage	Percentage	
Grammar, Punctuation and Spelling Test 1	/20			Good try! You need more practice in some topics – ask an adult to help you.
Grammar, Punctuation and Spelling Test 2	/20		**0–33%**	
Grammar, Punctuation and Spelling Test 3	/20			
Reading Test 1	/10			You're doing really well. Ask for extra help for any topics you found tricky.
Reading Test 2	/10		**34–69%**	
Reading Test 3	/10			
Reading Test 4	/10			You're a 10-Minute SATs Test star – good work!
Maths Set A: Test 1	/13		**70–100%**	
Maths Set A: Test 2				
Maths Set B: Test 1	/13			
Maths Set B: Test 2				
Maths Set C: Test 1	/13			
Maths Set C: Test 2				

You've taken your 10-minute tests...

now try a complete practice paper

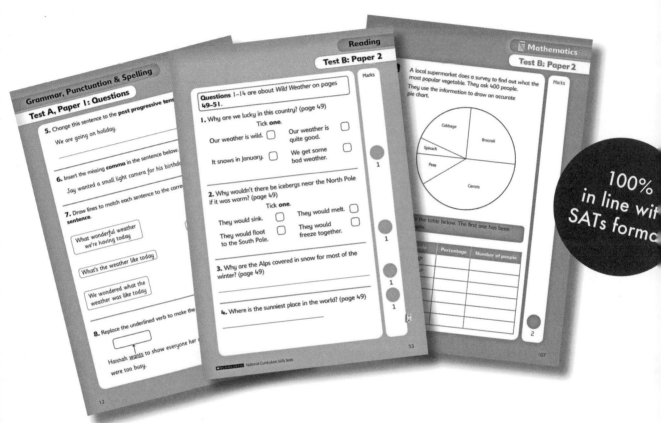

Prepare at home with authentic SATs practice tests

- Boost children's confidence with practice for maths, reading, and grammar, punctuation and spelling

- Format, question types and mark schemes exactly match the National Tests

- Covers key National Test topics for Year 2 to Year 6

- Each book includes up to three full practice tests, plus answers and advice*

*Two full test papers are included for Maths.

Find out more at www.scholastic.co.uk